ONE-MINUTE PUZZLES TO FUZZLE YOUR BRAIN

THE HIDDEN PICTURE CHALLENGE

BY ROBIN PREISS GLASSER

Lowell House
Juvenile
Los Angeles

CONTEMPORARY BOOKS
Chicago

For my father, with love, who
has never hidden his support.

Requests for such permissions should be addressed to:
Lowell House Juvenile
2029 Century Park East, Suite 3290
Los Angeles, CA 90067

Lowell House books can be purchased at special discounts
when ordered in bulk for premiums or special sales.
Contact Department VH at the above address.

Manufactured in the United States of America

ISBN: 1-56565-252-5

10 9 8 7 6 5 4 3 2 1

INTRODUCTION

If you dare, take the *One-Minute Puzzle* challenge. You'll have hours of fun solving these delightfully detailed dilemmas as you search for a host of hidden objects. But hurry—you only have a minute to solve each one!

THE WITCH'S BAKERY

1

The wicked witch is baking a vulture cake, but she has misplaced some utensils. Take no more than a minute to find her rolling pin, measuring cup, measuring spoons, and big wooden mixing spoon—before she casts a spell on you!

TOE-NAIL
FLOUR
SHAVINGS

2

The girl is so busy with her computer, she doesn't know that her pets have gotten out of their cages. In a minute or less, quickly help her find the canary, turtle, snake, mouse, and lizard—before her mom finds out!

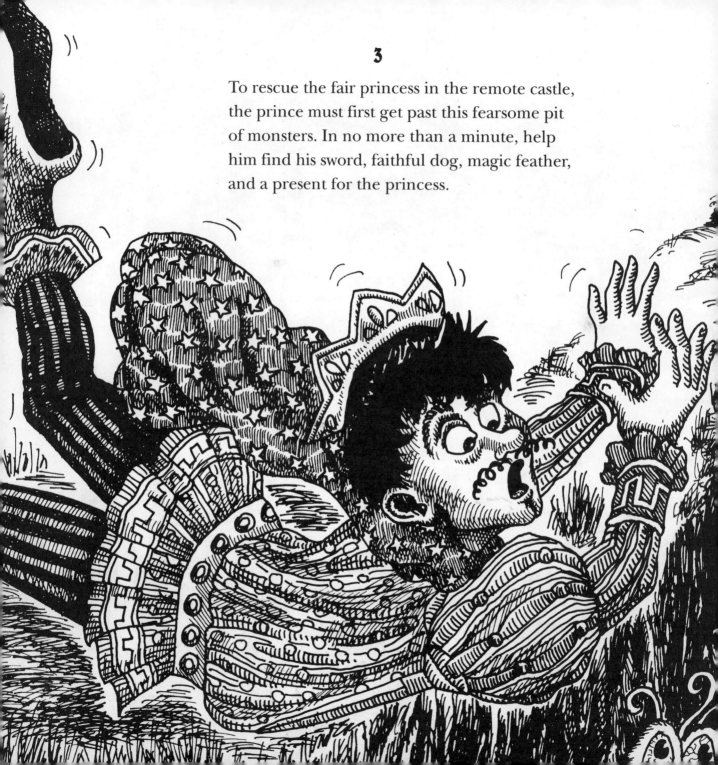

3

To rescue the fair princess in the remote castle, the prince must first get past this fearsome pit of monsters. In no more than a minute, help him find his sword, faithful dog, magic feather, and a present for the princess.

4

In her shopping frenzy, the woman has misplaced some of her *own* things. Take a minute or less to help her find her handbag, lipstick, beaded necklace, boot, and hairbrush.

5

This rowdy gang of pirates is posing for a portrait, but they've lost their pet birds. In one minute—before the photographer snaps the picture— help the pirates find Sam the seagull, Pete the parrot, and Toto the toucan.

6

The cat has surprised the cat
burglar. He has only one minute to
rob the house before the owners
come home. Since he can't see in
the dark, you can quickly save the
diamond ring, pearl necklace, silver
candlestick, and bag of money.

This seems like an ideal place to set up camp, but if you look carefully, there are hidden dangers lurking here. Take no more than a minute to find the bear, wolf, crocodile, bat, coyote, and snake— before it's too late!

8

In the excitement to finish their private clubhouse, the girls have lost their tools. In a minute or less, help them find the screwdriver, saw, hammer, pliers, and three screws.

NO BOYS ALLOWED!

GIRLS' CLUB

Hurry! Some animals at the zoo have escaped from
their cages. Help the zookeeper find the skunk,
penguin, koala, rabbit, and fish, but take no more
than a minute. The animals are in danger!

10

On Halloween night, the children mistakenly approach a house that's *really* haunted. In a minute or less, find the cat, pumpkin, witch's hat, flashlight, and candlestick.

Although the man is shipwrecked on this island, he could leave in a minute! You can show him where the rowboat, two oars, suitcase of new clothes, and chest full of gold are hidden.

12

The clever fox has outwitted the Royal
Hunting Party again, and the king's about
to take the plunge! In a minute or less, find
the bugle, gold pocket watch, bag of money,
and the king's Royal Glove.

13

Look carefully before you pick a
wildflower in this garden! Take no
more than a minute to find the
hidden dangers—a snake, two bees,
and a poisonous spider. Also look
for a harmless dragonfly.

The tide is coming in, and this family
has one minute to leave the beach.
Help them find their bottle of tanning
lotion, shovel, pail, starfish, soda can,
and missing sandal.

THE WILD RIDE!

The passengers on The Wild Ride want to get off! In a minute or less, find some foods the kids won't want to see when the ride comes to a stop—a hot dog, an ice-cream cone, a slice of pizza, a lollipop, and a box of popcorn.

16

Somebody opened the curtain before the
dancers were ready! The performance will
begin in one minute. Quickly find the lost
toe shoe, ballet slipper, tiara, wig, bouquet
of flowers, and hand mirror.

17

It's Christmas Eve, but the confused
Easter Bunny has arrived by mistake!
Before the children wake up, take no
more than a minute to find the Easter
basket, three Easter eggs, Easter bonnet,
and the two bunny helpers.

18

The mischievous ghosts in the
haunted mansion have played
a trick on the downstairs maid.
Take a minute or less to find
her broom, pail, mop, and
dust pan—before the mistress
of the house comes home.

19

While the odious ogre sleeps, the beautiful maiden plots her escape. Before the ogre wakes up, take no more than a minute to help her find the rope, the ogre's cane, and some bread and a flask of water for her long journey home.

20

This archaeologist has discovered a cave of living dinosaurs. Is it safe? she wonders. In a minute or less, help her locate clues to answer the question. Find the boot, hat, belt, glasses, and binoculars that belonged to a previous trespasser who disappeared.

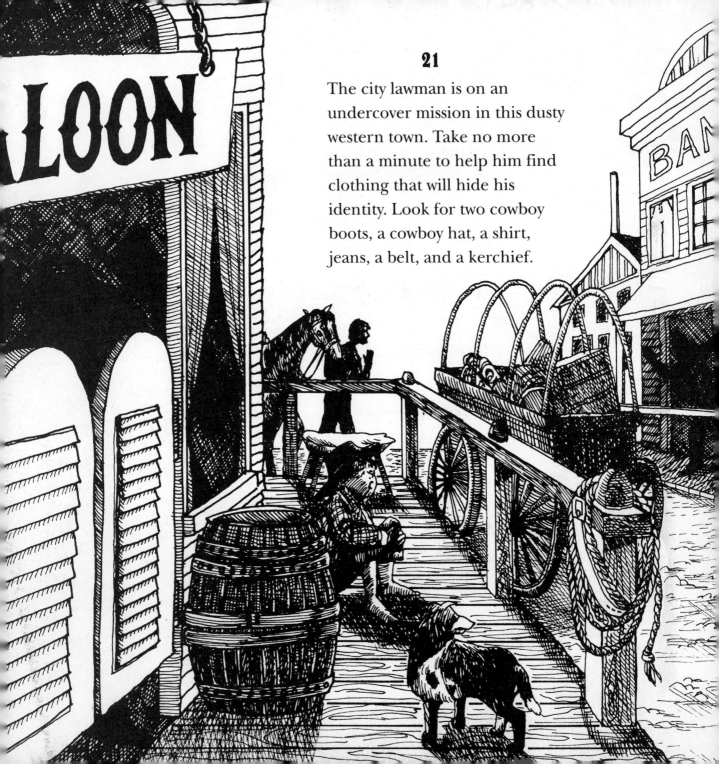

21

The city lawman is on an undercover mission in this dusty western town. Take no more than a minute to help him find clothing that will hide his identity. Look for two cowboy boots, a cowboy hat, a shirt, jeans, a belt, and a kerchief.

ANSWERS

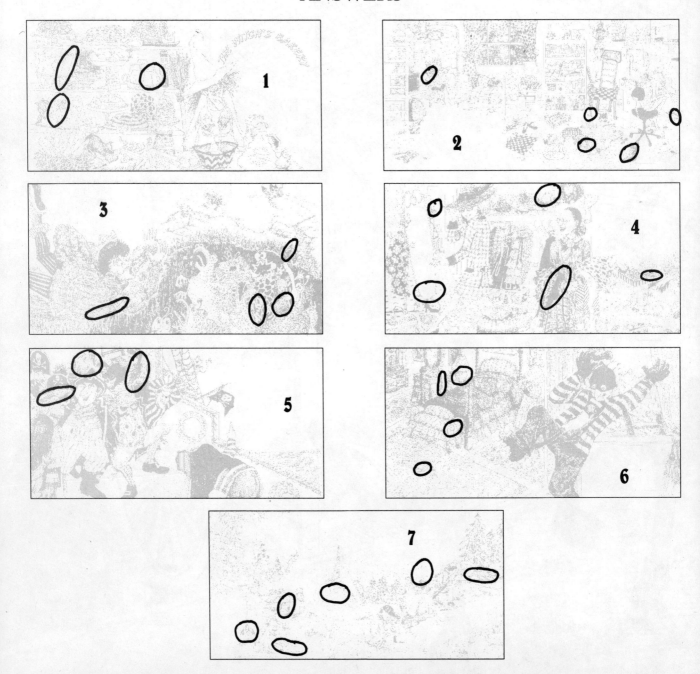

ANSWERS

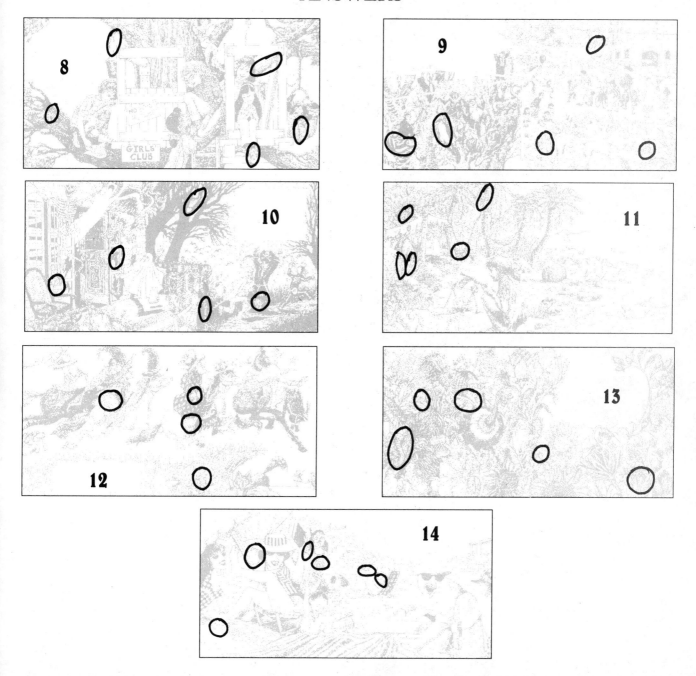

ANSWERS

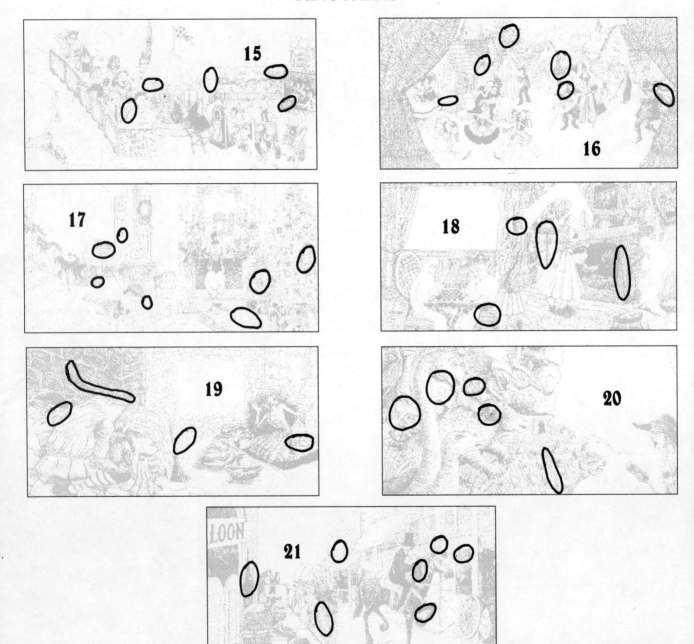